ISBN: 978-1-949474-72-5

Edition: March 2020

For all inquiries, please contact us at:
info@puppysmiles.org

To see more of our books, visit us at:
www.PuppyDogsAndIceCream.com

This book is given with love

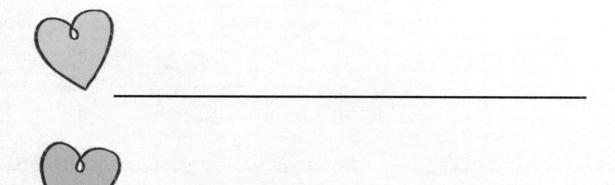

_____

_____

You've finally come home.
You're so tiny and sweet.
Now that you're here,
our family's complete.

The big grown-up bathtub
seems like an ocean,
as I help you get clean
with bubbles and lotion.

It's a bright, cheery day
and we're out for a stroll.
Our dog sits in back
and we're ready to roll!

A spoon and a bowl
are not just for baking.
In the right little hands
they create music-making.

Spring means beginnings,
everything's new.
Frog surprises mean more
'cause I share them with you.

Fingers or brushes?
Three colors or one?
Painting and choosing
are part of the fun.

My heart felt so sad
when you fell down today.
I hugged you and kissed you
and took the hurt away.

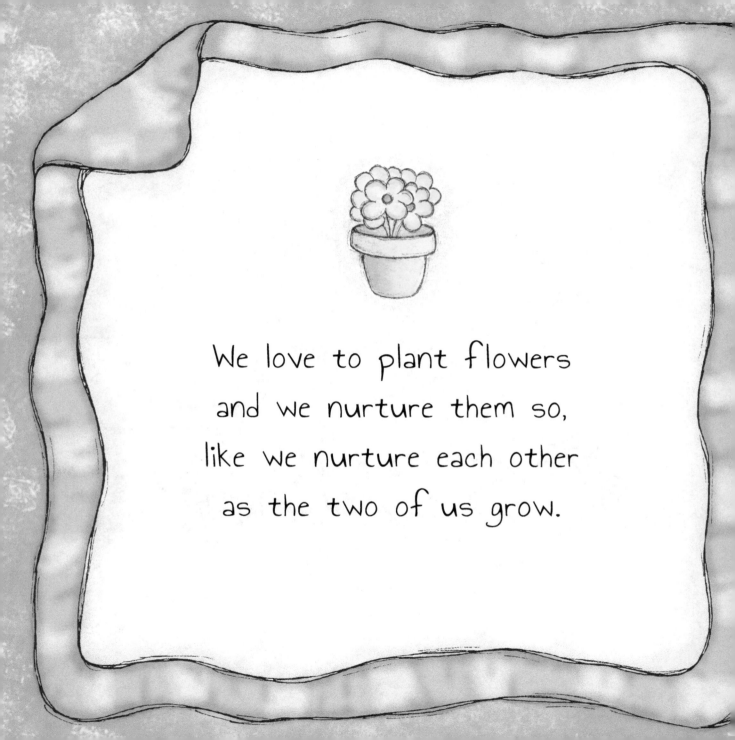

We love to plant flowers
and we nurture them so,
like we nurture each other
as the two of us grow.

And speaking of growing...
we just checked our chart.
I'm quite a bit taller
but I had a head start.

We're dipping our eggs
in the colors of spring,
the blue of the sky
and a baby chick's wing.

When the bugs crawl away,
my sister gets weepy,
but her "pets" must go free
so our home won't be creepy.

Summertime, summertime
the sun bronzes our skin.
Soon we'll race to the waves
and dip our toes in.

It's cozy and safe
as we lift up our prayers.
Our angel surrounds us.
Dreams soften our cares.

We look so ultra-stylish
when we wear ladies' clothes.
We feel very grown-up
from our heads to our toes.

SURPRISE! It's my birthday!
We eat gobs of pink cake,
rip open my gifts
and stay up way too late.

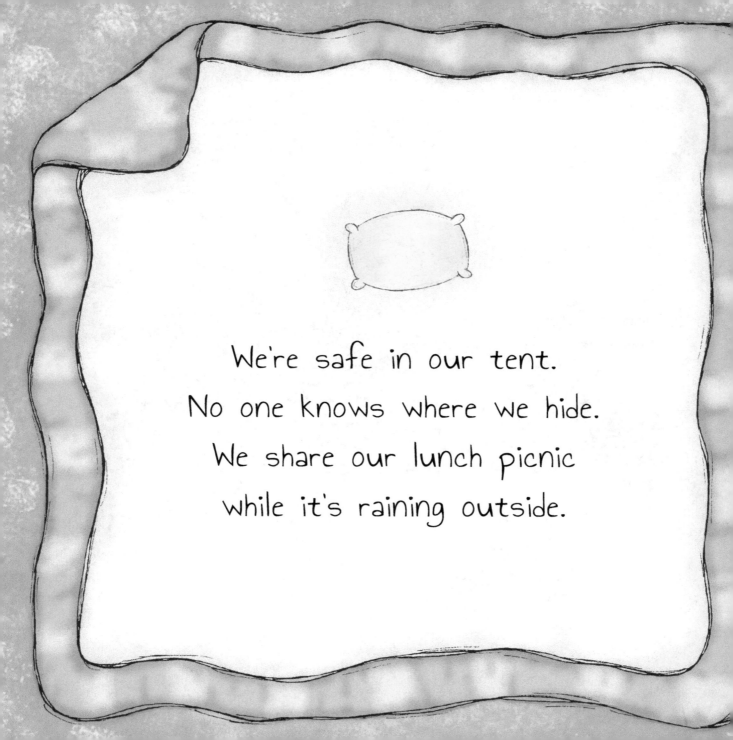

We're safe in our tent.
No one knows where we hide.
We share our lunch picnic
while it's raining outside.

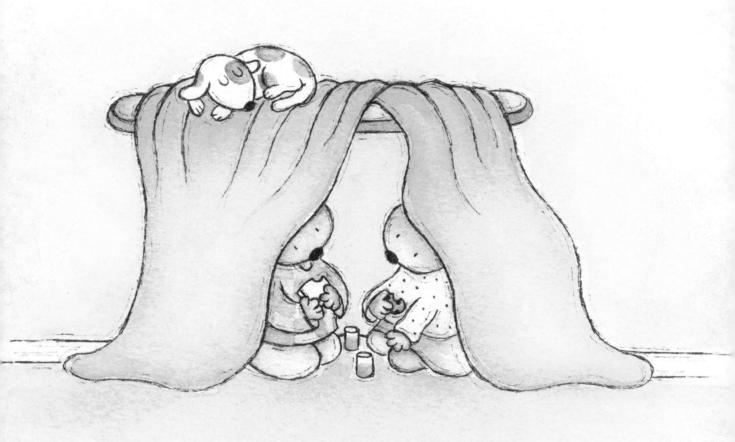

It's time to make magic
on this chilly fall night.
We carve plain orange pumpkins
into Halloween light.

We turn up our music
as loud as we dare.
Then we clap, sing, and dance
as we twirl in the air.

We've built our first snow bear
since last week's big storm.
Now we need steaming cocoa
to make cold sisters warm.

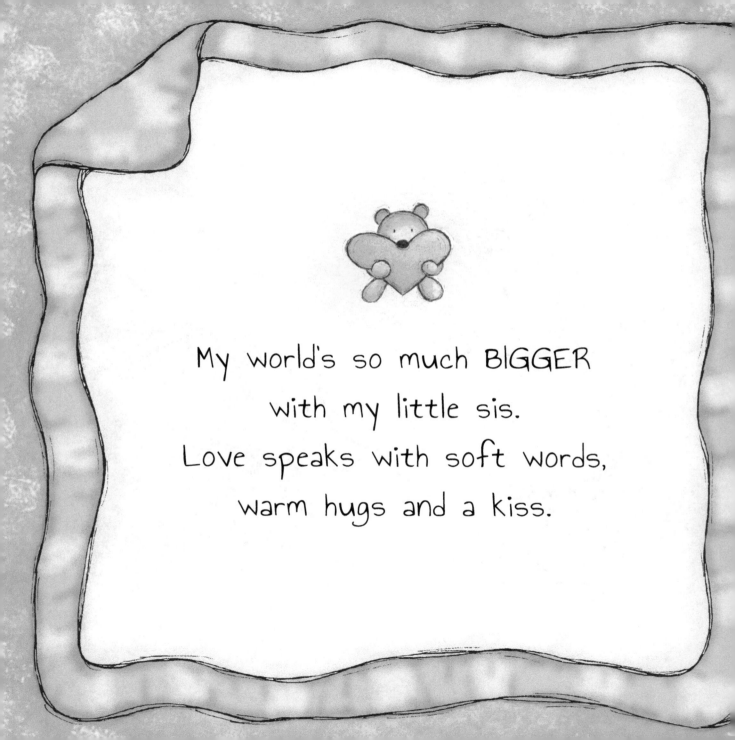

My world's so much BIGGER
with my little sis.
Love speaks with soft words,
warm hugs and a kiss.

CPSIA information can be obtained
at www.ICGtesting.com
Printed in the USA
BVHW011031211120
593844BV00001B/3